HAPPILY
EVER AFTER!

CONTENTS

THE PRINCESS
AND THE
PEA

Adapted by Carol Krueger
Illustrated by Helen Bacon

Narrator: Once upon a time, there was a young prince. His parents wanted him to get married.

Prince: But I don't want to. Weddings are so boring.

King: You have to, and you must marry a real princess. So we have a special test.

Queen: I'm going to put this pea under twenty mattresses. Only a real princess will feel the pea as she tries to sleep.

Narrator: So the king and queen invited some princesses to sleep on the special bed. The first princess arrived.

Princess Bob: I'm Boberella, but call me Princess Bob. This is my spider, Bill.

Narrator: From behind her long dress crept an enormous spider. He climbed up onto the royal bed.

Queen: Oh yuck! We have a dungeon for spiders!

Princess Bob: He's quite happy here. Now, if you don't mind, we're both tired. Good night.

7

 Narrator: The next morning, everybody came to see the princess.

 Queen: How did you sleep?

 Princess Bob: Bill and I slept just fine, thank you.

 Narrator: So Princess Bob and Bill were shown the way out.

The next princess was Princess Giggles. She came into the castle, giggling all the way. She climbed up the ladder to the top mattress and opened her trunk.

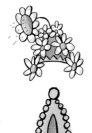 **Princess Giggles**: I'm putting this candy under my pillow.

 **Queen**: What for?

 Princess Giggles: So I'll have sweet dreams! Hee, hee, hee!

9

Narrator: Then Princess Giggles took out a box of games.

Princess Giggles: What's a snake's favorite English game

All: What?

Princess Giggles: Snakes and ladders! Hee, hee, hee!

Princess Giggles: Hey, this is my clock game. What do you get if you cross a watch with a crocodile?

All: What?

Princess Giggles: A clockodile! Hee, hee, hee!

Narrator: They left Princess Giggles to sleep and, in the morning, they saw her again.

Queen: How did you sleep?

Princess Giggles: Like a cat – *purrr*fectly! Hee, hee, hee!

Narrator: Princess Giggles left the palace still giggling.

Then Princess Lucy arrived. She had long, golden hair. She didn't have a spider, and she didn't giggle. In the morning, the queen spoke to her.

12

Queen: How did you sleep?

Princess Lucy: Not very well.
There was a lump in the bed.

13

King: Then you're a real princess!

Queen: A real treasure!

Prince: A real pain, too, because now I'll have to marry you!

Narrator: So, several years later, the prince and the real princess got married and lived happily ever after, *most* of the time!

The Rat Daughter

ADAPTED BY CAROL KRUEGER
ILLUSTRATED BY LORENZO VAN DER LINGEN

 **Narrator:** Mr. and Mrs. Rat had a beautiful daughter.

 **Mrs. Rat:** I think our daughter should marry the most powerful creature in the world.

 Mr. Rat: What a good idea! Who is the most powerful creature in the world?

 **Mrs. Rat:** Why, Sun, of course. Let's go talk to him.

Narrator: So Mr. and Mrs. Rat and their beautiful daughter went to speak to Sun.

Mr. Rat: We would like our beautiful daughter to marry the most powerful creature in the world. That is you.

Sun: Oh, I see. Yes, your daughter is very beautiful.

Narrator: But Sun did not want to marry a rat, even a good-looking one.

Sun: I am not really the most powerful creature in the world. Wind is. He is so powerful that he can race past me.

Mrs. Rat: You're right!
Thank you, Sun.
We'll go talk to him.

23

Narrator: So Mr. and Mrs. Rat and their beautiful daughter went to speak to Wind.

Mr. Rat: Wind, we would like our daughter to marry the most powerful creature in the world. That is you.

Narrator: Wind sighed through the grass. He thought the Rat Daughter was the most beautiful rat he had ever seen, but he didn't want to marry her.

Wind: I don't think I'm the most powerful creature in the world. Wall is, because, no matter how hard I try, I cannot blow him over.

 **Mrs. Rat:** Yes, you're right! We'll go talk to him.

 **Narrator:** So Mr. and Mrs. Rat and their beautiful daughter went to speak to Wall.

 Mr. Rat: Wall, we would like our daughter to marry the most powerful creature in the world. That is you.

 Narrator: Wall smiled. He thought that the Rat Daughter was very beautiful.

 Wall: I suppose I could marry her.

 **Narrator:** Just then, the Rat Daughter began to cry.

Rat Daughter: I don't want to marry *him*!

 Mr. Rat: But I insist that you marry the most powerful creature in the world.

 Wall: Do you know that there is someone even more powerful than I am?

 **All:** Who?

 Wall: That rat there!

 Narrator: Out from behind Wall came a handsome young rat.

Wall: He is more powerful than I am, because he has strong teeth. He can nibble through me and make me fall!

Handsome Rat: I would be happy to marry her.

Rat Daughter: I would be happy to marry him.

29

Mr. Rat and Mrs. Rat:
We would be happy to have our daughter marry the most powerful creature in the world!

Narrator: So the Rat Daughter and the Handsome Rat had a wonderful wedding and lived happily ever after!

FROM THE AUTHOR

I love happy endings, and one of the most wonderful things about being a writer is that you can have people live happily ever after!

Carol Krueger

FROM THE ILLUSTRATORS

In my garden, I grow sweet peas, but I'd really like a garden like the king and queen's, with lots of trees cut into unusual shapes.

Helen Bacon

I like drawing stories that have elements of fantasy or magic in them, and the best magic of all is a happy ending!

Lorenzo Van Der Lingen

If you have enjoyed reading
Happily Ever After!
read these other Storyteller Chapter Books.

Crazy Miss Maisey's Alphabet Pets
The Flutey Family Fruitcake
Rupert Goes to School
Feathers
Coyote, Fox, and Wolf Tales
3, 2, 1... Liftoff!
No Space to Waste
The Masterpiece
Those Birds!
Pandora's Box
Sam's Dad
Birds of Prey
Bird Watchers
Zoom In!
Clever Coyote and Other Wild Dogs
Trees, Please!
Solve This!